D0055640

BROWN & FRIENDS

I LOVE YOU
BEARY MUCH

LINE FRIENDS

©LINE

Cover design by Ching N. Chan.

Hachette Book Group supports the right to free expression and the value of copyright. The purpose of copyright is to encourage writers and artists to produce the creative works that enrich our culture.

The scanning, uploading, and distribution of this book without permission is a theft of the author's intellectual property. If you would like permission to use material from the book (other than for review purposes), please contact permissions@hbgusa.com. Thank you for your support of the author's rights.

Little, Brown and Company
Hachette Book Group
1290 Avenue of the Americas, New York, NY 10104
Visit us at LBYR.com
linefriends.com

First Edition: October 2021

Little, Brown and Company is a division of Hachette Book Group, Inc. The Little, Brown name and logo are trademarks of Hachette Book Group, Inc.

The publisher is not responsible for websites (or their content) that are not owned by the publisher.

Library of Congress Control Number 2021934876

ISBNs: 978-0-316-16795-6 (paper over board), 978-0-316-30475-7 (ebook), 978-0-316-28697-8 (ebook), 978-0-316-30458-0 (ebook)

Printed in the United States of America

PHX

10 9 8 7 6 5 4 3 2 1

BROWN & FRIENDS
I LOVE YOU BEARY MUCH
A Little Book of Happiness

Jenne Simon

Little, Brown and Company
New York Boston

LINE FRIENDS

LOVE. It makes the sun shine and the birds sing and gives you the warm fuzzies deep down inside. It's a feeling of pure joy and connection. But what does love look like? And how does it feel? **BROWN & FRIENDS** know the secret!

    BROWN is a bona fide sweetheart. He'll do anything for **CONY** in the name of love; showers his sister, **CHOCO**, with affection; and cherishes chillin' with his friends **SALLY**, **LEONARD**, **EDWARD**, and the rest of the gang. Because he knows how beary special all different kinds of love can be.

    So, whether you're in search of a little romance, are excited to bond with your besties, or are learning how to love yourself, **BROWN & FRIENDS** are here to show you just how special opening your heart to love can be.

CHAPTER 1

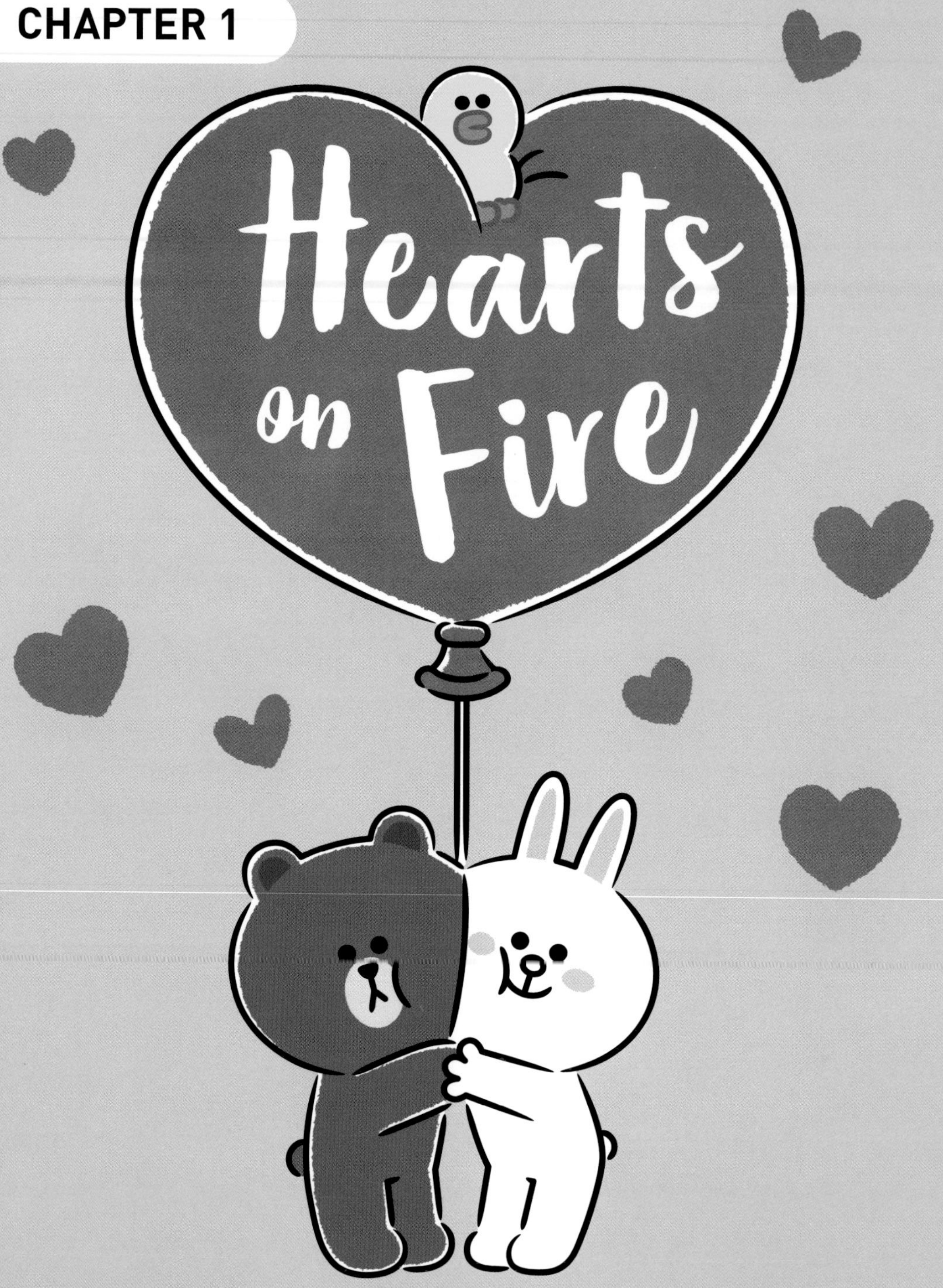

That special
someone is
out there...
waiting for
you.

When you see them,
YOU MAY FEEL
LIKE YOU'VE BEEN
SHOT
by
Cupid's arrow.

Does your heart feel fizzy? ✔

Does your head feel dizzy? ✔

Are butterflies flitting around inside you? ✔

Do you wonder if they feel those feelings, too? ✔ ✔ ✔

EVERY MOMENT WITH THAT SPECIAL SOMEONE CAN FEEL LIKE A GIFT. ONE THAT'S WORTH TREASURING.

WHEN YOU FIND YOUR PERFECT MATCH,

BE PLAYFUL,
BE PATIENT,
BE KIND.
AND REMEMBER THAT
LOVE ISN'T A GAME.

True love
is written
in the stars!

CHAPTER 2

BEST
FRIENDS
FOREVER

LOVE ISN'T ONLY ABOUT ROMANCE. IT CAN BE SHARED BETWEEN TRUE FRIENDS.

THE KIND WHO REALLY GET YOU.

Adventures are more fun with your BFFs, whether you are:

Cruising around ✔

Spending a night on the town ✔

Shopping at the mall ✔

Or doing nothing at all ✔ ✔ ✔

You can find best friends anywhere...even in your own family!

When times get tough, friends lend a hand.

YOU CAN SUPPORT ONE ANOTHER BY GIVING ADVICE AND TAKING IT, TOO.

BECAUSE YOU'RE ON **THE SAME TEAM.**

Friends tell one another their secrets.

And listen to one another's fears.

There is **no one** you'd rather be stranded with.

And **no one** better to help you achieve your

dreams.

And when besties get together, it's a

P-A-R-T-Y!

#squadgoals

CHAPTER 3

LOVING YOURSELF

YOU KNOW WHO KNOWS YOU BEST? You do!

AND IT'S OKAY TO SHOW YOURSELF A LITTLE LOVE. IN FACT, it's a must!

Do you want time for yourself? ✔

How about a little luxury? ✔

Or to raise your voice and be heard? ✔

You deserve all that and more. ✔ ✔ ✔

Need some Me Time? Take it!

Self-care is self-love.
It feeds your body
and your soul...

so take a minute to stop
and smell the roses.

SOAK UP THE SUN!
RELAX AND
LET ALL THOSE
GOOD VIBES IN.

YOU DO YOU.
FIND WHAT YOU LOVE,
THEN MAKE TIME FOR IT.
HAPPINESS IS
FOR EVERYONE.

LIFE IS SWEETEST
WHEN YOU'RE AS KIND
TO YOURSELF

AS YOU ARE
WITH OTHERS.

CHAPTER 4

LOVING LIFE

Life is an adventure.
There are surprises around
every corner and fun to be
had wherever you go.

LOVE EVERY
MINUTE OF IT!

Translation? It's okay to go a little wild sometimes. Let your **INNER ANIMAL** come out to play. And don't be afraid to let yourself

Live every day out loud!

Because
though time passes
in the blink of an eye...
memories are forever.
Make yours mean
something.

And don't forget to celebrate special moments.

Toast your triumphs ✔

Blow your own horn ✔

Make a splash ✔

WORK HARD.

PLAY
HARDER.

LIFE AND LOVE
ARE NOT FOR
THE FAINT OF HEART.

AND WHATEVER YOU DO,

LET LOVE
BE YOUR GUIDE!

LOVE,
BROWN & FRIENDS